D1015530

Dog and Cat Shake a Leg

A Viking Easy-to-Read

Kate Spohn

VIKING

FRIENDS

Dog and Cat are out for a walk.

They see their friend Goose.

"Hello, Goose!" say Dog and Cat.

"Hello, Dog! Hello, Cat!" says Goose.

"Where are you going?"

"We are going for a walk," says Dog.

"Please join us," says Cat.

So Dog, Cat, and Goose walk together.

2

They see Mouse.

"Hello, Mouse!" they all say.

"Hello, friends!" says Mouse.

Mouse joins them.

The four friends walk together.

They see a sign.
It says:

COME ONE,
COME ALL.
SEE US DANCE.
HAVE A BALL!

"I once took dance lessons," says Goose.

"So did I," says Mouse.
"Dancing is fun!" says Cat.
"Let's go!" says Dog.
So Dog and Cat
and Goose and Mouse go
to see the dance.

The dancers do amazing leaps and spins.

"Hee, hee, hee!" laughs Cat.
"Ha, ha, ha!" laughs Dog.
Goose laughs, too.
And so does Mouse.

Now *everyone* is laughing and dancing
and having a ball!

THE HAT

Cat is looking for a new hat.
"I don't know what kind of hat
I want," she tells Dog.
"Then I will go with you
and help you decide," says Dog.

At the hat shop,
Cat tries on a cowboy hat.

"That looks great!" Dog says.
"I *love* cowboy hats!"
"No," says Cat.
"This hat does not feel right."

Cat tries on a beret next.
"You look like an artist,"
Dog tells Cat.
"No," says Cat.
"This hat is not for me."

Cat tries on a baseball hat.
It is too small.

"How about a top hat?" says Dog.
"A top hat is very nice."

Cat tries on a top hat.
It is too tall.

Dog picks up a floppy hat.
"How about a sombrero?" he asks.
Cat tries on the sombrero.
"I feel silly," says Cat.

"Well, what about this straw hat?" asks Dog.
Cat tries on the straw hat.

It is not too big. It is not too small.
It is not too tall. It is not too silly.
"I love it!" Cat says.

Dog waits outside
while Cat buys her hat.

"I'd like to buy this straw hat,"
Cat tells the shopkeeper.
Then Cat whispers something
to the shopkeeper.

13

When Cat comes outside
she has two hatboxes.
In one box is the straw hat.
In the other box is—the cowboy hat!

"Cat, you shouldn't have," Dog says.
"I was happy to do it," says Cat.

Dog and Cat look fine in their new hats.

HOMEBODY

It is morning.

Dog is at home.

He is reading.

"It is so nice to be at home," Dog says.

Dog is in his pajamas.

"I think I will stay in my
pajamas all day," he says.

Dog makes up a song.

"Home, home.
Home is sweet.
With pajamas
and a book
and a bone to eat."

17

Knock! Knock!

Cat is knocking on Dog's door.

"Come on in," says Dog.

"Come on in and read with me."

"No, Dog," says Cat.

"You come on out.

It is a beautiful morning!"

Dog looks out his window.

He goes to his door
and steps onto his porch.

The sun is shining.

The birds are singing.

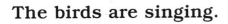

And the air is mild and breezy.
Dog says, "Cat, you are right.
"It *is* a beautiful morning outside.
But it is a beautiful morning inside, too."

Cat looks around Dog's house.
The windows are open.
A vase is filled with spring flowers.

There are books on the table
and pillows on the sofa.

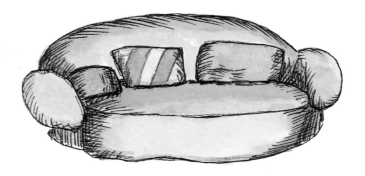

Cat says, "You are right, too, Dog.
It *is* a beautiful morning inside!"

So Cat comes in and sits
next to Dog on the sofa.
Together they read and enjoy
being inside on a nice day.

TRIED AND TRUE

AND SOMETHING NEW

Dog and Cat are on their way
to get ice cream.
As they walk they think
of their favorite flavors.
Dog's favorite flavor is vanilla.
But Cat has *two* favorite flavors.
"I can't decide," says Cat.
"How about a scoop of each," says Dog.
"That way you can have
both your favorite flavors."

So that is what Cat does.
At the ice cream shop, Cat gets
one scoop of strawberry,
and one scoop of mint chocolate chip.

Dog and Cat sit on their favorite bench
to eat their ice cream.

Along comes Goose.

She is on Rollerblades.

"Hello, Goose!" they say.

"Hello, Dog! Hello, Cat!" says Goose.

Dog and Cat see Mouse.
Mouse is Rollerblading, too!
"Hello, Mouse!" they all say.
"Hello, Dog! Hello, Cat!
Hello, Goose!" says Mouse.

"You will never catch *me* on Rollerblades!"
Cat tells Dog.
"Me either!" says Dog.
Cat is glad that her friend is so smart—
just like she is.

A few days later,
Dog and Cat are out on a walk.
Cat tells Dog about a dream she had.
"Last night," says Cat,
"I dreamed we were Rollerblading."
"No!" says Dog.
"Yes!" says Cat.
"Maybe we should try it," says Dog.
"Yes, let's go Rollerblading," says Cat.

And that is what they do.

Dog and Cat go to town.

They rent Rollerblades and put them on.

"Shake a leg!" says Cat.

"Away we go!" says Dog.

Dog falls down.

Cat falls down, too.

But they get back up,

and soon they have the hang of it.

Dog and Cat see Goose and Mouse.
Goose and Mouse are Rollerblading, too.
"Come skate with us," says Goose.
Dog and Cat join them.
The four friends Rollerblade together.
And away they all go!

To my dear friend Eugene.

Howdy-do?

Very well.
Thanks for asking!

VIKING
Published by the Penguin Group
Penguin Books USA Inc., 375 Hudson Street, New York, New York 10014, U.S.A.
Penguin Books Ltd, 27 Wrights Lane, London W8 5TZ, England
Penguin Books Australia Ltd, Ringwood, Victoria, Australia
Penguin Books Canada Ltd, 10 Alcorn Avenue, Toronto, Ontario, Canada M4V 3B2
Penguin Books (N.Z.) Ltd, 182–190 Wairau Road, Auckland 10, New Zealand

Penguin Books Ltd, Registered Offices: Harmondsworth, Middlesex, England

First published in 1996 by Viking, a division of Penguin Books USA Inc.

3   5   7   9   10   8   6   4   2

Copyright © Kate Spohn, 1996
All rights reserved ·

LIBRARY OF CONGRESS CATALOGING-IN-PUBLICATION DATA
Spohn, Kate.   Dog and Cat shake a leg / [text and illustrations] by Kate Spohn.
p.   cm.—(Viking easy-to-read)
Summary: Two best friends, Dog and Cat, have fun together when they dance,
shop for hats, eat ice cream, read, and rollerblade.
ISBN 0-670-86758-6
[1. Dogs—Fiction. 2. Cats—Fiction. 3. Friendship—Fiction.]
I. Title. II. Series.
PZ7.S7636Do 1996   [E]—dc20   95-23724 CIP AC

Printed in Singapore   Set in New Century Schoolbook

Viking® and Easy-to-Read® are registered trademarks of Penguin Books USA Inc.

Reading level 1.8